GRANT to GRANT

aka GRANT and ASSOCIATES

(LIFE AFTER WASHINGTON)

"CHAMPAGNE AND A DRAM OF POISON"

(SUBTITLE: REMEMBERING WHAT WAS…

(SCANDAL IN DE KALB, COUNTY)

Murder, Greed, and Rape

Revenge and retribution…a shadow falls over the city…causes terror in the town and County

Another episode for GRANT AND ASSOCIATES

Champagne and Dram of POISON:

Remember What Was

Imogene Grant

Zeta Publishing, Inc
3850 SE 58th Ave
Ocala, FL 34480
www.zetapublishing.com

This is a work of fiction. All of the characters, names, incidents, organizations, and dialogue in this novel are either the products of the author's imagination or are used fictitiously.

Any similarity to anyone living or dead is purely coincidental and not to be believed.

Ordering Information:
Quantity sales. Special discounts are available on quantity purchases by corporations, associations, and others. For details, contact the publisher at the address above.
Orders by U.S. trade bookstores and wholesalers. Please contact Zeta Publishing: Tel: (352) 694-2553; Fax: (352) 694-1791 or visit www.zetapublishing.com

Rev. Date: May 2020

ISBN: 978-1-950340-10-1 (sc)
ISBN: 978-1-950340-11-8 (e)

Library of Congress: 2019918764
Printed in the United States of America

THEME: An act of vengeance…

LOCALE: SOME WHERE IN A LARGE CITY

SOURCE: The fertile mind of Imogene Starks Grant.

GENRE: MURDER MELO DRAMA…RETROBUTION, WEALTH by
any means IS NEVER AN EXCUSE:

FADE IN:

EXT: THE STREETS AND PARK_ AT TWILIGHT

COUPLES AMBLED ALONG, LOVERS CUDLED on benches and others
on blankets SOUNDS OF TWILIGHT IN THE CITY… AUTOMOBILES
horns AND OTHER FAMILIAR NIGHT NOISES.

Suddenly an explosion ripped the quiet of the darkness …followed by
explosions after explosion, people running screaming, cars, buses and
trucks careened and slammed into the sides of buildings, fire hydrants
sprays geysers of water, awning from sidewalk cafes sail through the streets,
plate glass shatters and people are buried as the walls tumbled down,
people jumping from the floors above, a baby tossed to the fireman below,
children's cry…fiery black clouds of smoke seen for miles away, firefighters
from surrounding cities the seeming extermination of the citizens, a harsh
reminder to some of an attack of war…six square city blocks of prime real
estate blown to rubble.

Looky loos are kept away from workmen, and their grim task of separating
dead flesh from the debris, ambulances and any rescue vehicles… The
Mayor and other city Council moved around the grotesque sight.

NEWSCASTER excited, saying "One woman struck down by falling bricks...The man carried her through the flames to the outside, where firemen took his burden, firemen extinguish his smoldering clothes.

EXT: PILES OF RUBBLE- DAY

Day dawned…six square city blocks appeared like a war zone as workmen toiled feverishly to clear the

Rubble, searching for the dead and dying and any survivor… bodies were carried out and the dead was wrapped and stacked like wood. Fire fighters worked through the burned areas for hot spots.

INT: NEWSCAST OF BOMBED AREA _ DAY

FLASHBACK:

NEWSCASTER said "After hours of searching two lone survivors carefully taken from the rubble and whisked off to the nearest hospital. Ladies and gentlemen what you are about to see is brutally graphic…not for innocent eyes…"

Newsmen, cameramen, police, looky Lou's, the grieving, sadness on the faces as rescuers grapple with the daunting task at hand.

FLASH BACK:

The film showed …The figure of a man his clothes in flames…carrying an unconscious woman. He turned the woman over to the rescuers…who extinguished the smoldering fire on his back.

 NEWSCASTER continued said, "It was reported the man carrying the unconscious woman is her twin brother he carried his unconscious twin sister through the falling stones and flames. He suffered second and third degree burns to his back and neck. He is now in MERCY HOSPITAL in deep depression …his sister is comatose due to falling bricks that fractured her skull …We will report any changes as the news arise."

LATER:

INT: NEWS ROOM - DAY

A news reporter stares into the teleprompter saying,

"I must report this morning an act of heroism during the firebombing in KINGS TOWN last night…A brother carried his unconscious sister through the flames and falling ruble even though his clothes were on fire. Can you imagine the agony this survivor suffered? His sister remains comatose at Mercy General Emergency Hospital; the brother survived sank into a deep depression…due to the enormity of the traumatic situation…We will keep you up to date as the news arises…"

The screen went to black…

INT: GRANT BEDROOM- DAY

LIV AND FITZ watch the news.

He kissed her lightly on the forehead, saying "Good morning."

Liv asked, "What was that?"

FITZ answered, saying "A kiss…and good morning why?"

"The love is gone… no oomph, missed the mark by at least eight inches"

LIV answered.

"If you don't know I didn't do it right…come here woman…" Fitz held her really tight as they became engrossed in the smooch of the century…

LIV was breathless when it was over saying, "WOW…" …"

Fitz asked, "Is that better?...Don't you know I love you more than anyone… to hold you like this, to kiss you and feel your body, warm and soft close to me everything about you is intoxicating."

LIV answered breathlessly, saying, "My man…you're my stuff… Now that's what I'm talk in 'bout." As she rested her head on his chest… continuing softly, "You had me at 'I love you' and I do love you more than you will ever know…"

They stood in the warm cocoon of their bodies.

FITZ said proudly, "The old guy ain't dead yet."

FIVE YEARS AFTER THE FIRE:

INT: HOSPITAL ROOM – NIGHT

A lone figure stood in the shadows at Andrea's bedside, a scared hand held hers saying in a harsh whisper, "I have to leave now sis but you will be taken care of while I'm gone…" he turns to go with a moan and a catch in his throat, he looks back at the door for one last view of Andrea.

EXT: NEWS HEADLINE ON STACK OF PAPERS, LATER

PAPERS ON A STREET CORNER – DAY

"DEPRESSED PATIENT, VICTIM OF THE EXPLOSION IN DE KALB COUNTY five years ago has disappeared without a trace… More when the news arises…" Newscaster excited continues, "This just in Ladies and Gentlemen… a body just found believe to be the patient that disappeared… he was burned beyond recognition…It was apparent the car he was driving ran off a cliff and exploded into flames, it burned so hot the remains were not recognizable as human…it's with sadness we will follow this story as it unfolds…"

INT: MEDICAL EXAMINERS OFFICE - DAY

WEEKS LATER:

DR. DAVIS Medical Examiner…having a pleasant discussion with his old friend… DR. DILLARD CHRYSLER.

DILLARD asked, "What's happening in the investigation of the bombing 'of six square blocks' in DE Kalb…how's their search for the missing burn patient progressing?"

DAVIS answered, "Nothing has happened…too much power in the cover up…It's called planning ahead lots of money changed hands …they wanted that particular property badly… as for the patient he healed nicely his clothes were actually burned into his back… with sedation the second and third degree …the skin peeled off all the char like an orange…he was sedated when he disappeared… I haven't a clue how he managed with all the trauma he suffered the last five years."

DR. DILLARD said, "Big money that's the problem …Did you hear the nurses are seeing a figure of a man and eerie shadows on Andrea's hospital floor …especially at night?"

DR. Davis replied laughing, "…Yes and they call him Andy back to look after his sister….Dillard don't tell me you believe the dead can return… Maybe he sends fresh flowers daily…I never saw that haunting side of you."

DILLARD answered, "No I don't think so… I think Andrew is still alive… when you said the car burned hot and the remains were burned to a cinder… not even the teeth could be harvested… I knew somehow it was Andrew… he never died in that car crash."

DAVIS replied, "HOW? I know that body was toast." he paused momentarily…Then continued, "You know the nurses think Andrea will wake up because she moans, her body twitches, muscular movement, she opens her eyes… although she does not focus."

"The body was toast but it was not Andrew… He would be close to her body because he took care of her while she was up and around… Andrea was his identical twin totally alike." DILLARD paused momentarily… Then continued, "Their father was an herbalist and had numerous patents…you probably use his tooth paste, teas, or rat poison and many more…. Uncle Ben taught his children everything…That is why Andrew is still alive… bank on it… Uncle Ben's patents were all bankable."

Davis chuckled saying, "That remains to be seen." laughing out loud.

DILLARD said, "It's true."

Davis answered, "That is for me to see… him in life not as a shadow or figure at the end of a hall."

DILLARD stood saying, "I don't know how or when but you'll see… I've got patients waiting … I'll be in touch with you later." As he left the room.

TEN YEARS GOES BY:

INT: TELEIVION 10 P.M. NEWS

NEWS CASTER …SAYING IN SOLUIM TONES…

"The only survivor of the bombing ten years ago expired at nine P.M. she never awoke from the coma…no apparent family members were at the bed side." he pauses momentarily, then in an excited voice, said, "We have breaking news Ladies and Gentlemen…the comatose victim… expired while giving birth to a stillborn child… this information by an anonymous source…flyers appeared on newsstands hours ago. According to our information the comatose patient was apparently raped by one of her caretakers…flyers were sent to the Mayor and scattered around the city. DNA tests are being done as we speak…male caretakers and any male employees past and present are being tested…

EXT: CEMETERY – NIGHT

A lone figure cast a tall shadow over the grave sites mother beside the smaller one… a scarred, shaky hand touched the head stone…a moan and quick intake of breath broke the silence of the night.

A harsh raspy whisper, "ANDRÉA VAUGHN mother DANIEL VAUGHN a child she will never know."

INT: D.N.A. LAB –NIGHT

A dark figure moves with a flash light quietly searching with scared hands… through files…until he finds the one he is looking for…he moves quickly photographing the files and leaves surreptitiously through the hall and disappeared into the darkness of an alley.

INT: UPSCALE DINING ROOM__NIGHT

'Tipplers Club's monthly meeting' and the wives night out.'

Today is HORACE JACOBS hosted' the man's only dinner and tippler delights….He stood saying, "I hope you like the nights offering. I gave it a lot of thought...First a light dinner wine to tickle your appetite. Bon Appétit ya'll." laughter follows the salute.

LATER AFTER DINNER:

CALVIN EVANS said loosening his belt, "Oh man that was a great dinner and the drinks … not too shabby…" laughing.

"We can have our Champagne to top the evening off in the living room… during the clean up… before the little women get back from their night out…" HORACE said leading the way….

INT: LIVING ROOM - NIGHT

Quiet conversation, the clicking of fluted glasses, a

Piano and Violin medley of soothing songs served as background.

The Champagne glasses were empty when the first chest pain struck Horace causing him to cry out… then one after another were writhing in excruciating pain….Their bodies twitched in death… one threw up on the carpet.

Their wives discovered the six dead men strewn about the living room.

Police converged on the home with full investigative crew, laboratory, and fingerprint men…they found the cleanup had been done thoroughly … left were place settings that exclaimed done…

It all started with this group of death

PLACE SETTINGS ARRANGED ON THE TABLE.

'CHAMPAIGNE AND A DRAM OF POISON' 'MAY ALL YOUR REGRETS BE IN HELL'.

Place cards were collected separately…along with a flyer that read follow the money the bombing was bought in De Kalb county.

INT: POLICE HEAD QARTERS__DAY

TOM JOHNSON enters and said, "We found someone who saw the caterers van at the Jacobs home… the caterer was a woman."

GEORGE SANDS asked, "After the dinner?"

TOM asked, "Did anyone describe her?"

GEORGE answered, "Yes she is on the way here now… but there is one catch."

TOM said sarcastically, "There always is… what is the catch… she has bad teeth… homeless what is the catch… make it good."

GEORGE answered, "She's partially blind… thirty percent of her sight left."

TOM laughed, "That's bad… what can she tell us?"

GEORGE replied saying, "It's not as bad as it sounds … she has thirty percent of her sight and takes her walks outside the Jacobs home every evening."

Cell phone sounds TOM answered listens, said,
"Take her to interrogation one… thanks…"

To George he said, "You heard she's here."

They leave the squad room.

INTERRIGATION ROOM ONE__DAY

An attractive young woman sat waiting… as the detectives entered placed their folders on the table.

TOM said, "You're Ms. HELEN CARTER…?

(She acknowledges with a nod)

The detective continued saying, "I'm Detective TOM Johnson and this is my pardoner GEORGE SANDS…"

 George asked, "I see you have a cane for the sight impaired…how much vision do you have?"

HELEN replied, "To the point… I like that…. I have thirty percent of my vision."

"What can you tell us about the night in question?" TOM asked.

HELEN said, "That was the night Mr. Jacobs had his usual dinner party…"

GEORGE said, "You knew about them?"

"Yes … everyone in the neighborhood know… we figured it was his turn… there are several in that 'TIPPLER CLUB' they take turns." HELEN said as a matter of fact.

GEORGE asked, "What can you tell us … did you see anything that might help us?"

HELEN replied, "Yes the party was breaking up when I took my usual walk about that time… a woman put away the equipment climbed into the caterers van as I waited at the end of the driveway for the van to pass."

TOM asked, "Could you see her face anything?"

"Writing on the van was COUNTRY COOKING… I think Mr. Jacobs and some in the group are founders of that company… cooking is quite good Southern Style." HELEN responded.

GEORGE said, "Could you see what the woman looked like…. white, black, tall, and short… what?"

"She wore a little French Maid out fits, showed lot of her legs… I thought she seemed very tall quite large for that get up… she could have been anything from white to light Hispanic…about five feet nine or ten inches tall… and I do remember one odd thing she wore those little white frilly gloves as she drove away."

TOM said, "You saw a lot…this is great…"

"Yes I did … I stood beside the driveway as she finished loading the van… I was in no hurry." HELEN said.

GEORGE asked, "She was alone to handle the pots and other things used for a party?"

HELEN answered, "That didn't appear to be a problem for her… there didn't seem to be food in the containers… and the carts were on wheels… I enjoyed just watching for a few minutes and she didn't mind… matter of fact she smiled at me as she worked."

TOM said, "Ms. Carter that seems to be it for the moment… we will contact you if we have more questions… Sergeant Donnelly will show you out and take you home… thanks for coming and your information is very helpful."

Donnelly guided Helen to the door.

GEORGE asked, "Did we hear from the Medical Examiner?"

"No not yet… let's take another look at the video." TOM said…he continues, "There is a Doctor DILLARD CRYSLER with a theory on the deaths… he's probably another know it all kook."

VIOLIN music played in the background…George started the video it… shows five dead men in differing positions in death, and the one still alive as he writhed in excruciating pain …the medical examiner administered oxygen and the necessary first aide, then said, "…Have some uniforms go with him…The vomiting probably helped. … Get him to the nearest emergency room code three… one of you stay at his side."

Neighbors and other looky Lou's gather on the side walk to see what was happening… all on camera.

The ambulance siren wailed as it sped through the streets of the city that night.

INT: MEDICAL EXAMINERS OFFICE__DAY

DR. DAVIS and CHRYSLER waited

Dr. DAVIS saying to police detectives, "I ask Dr. CHRYSLER over to observe me while I did the autopsy… We have to take our time on these deaths … they died in the same manner from essential elements that are found normally in the human body… the killer has made a cocktail… when given in just the right amounts can cause a horrible death."

DR. Chrysler said, "I have seen several similar deaths in the past few years… not recognized as the same method used because they are in different towns and other circumstances."

TOM asked, "Are you saying we're dealing with revenge or serial murders?"

DR. Chrysler responded, "I am saying just that… it took know how to concoct this exact formula… and you are also dealing with a hatred you've never seen before… not to mention one who knows the human body and how it works…" another thing, "Where did the money for Andrea to be kept in a private cottage with nurses around the clock, and fresh flowers every day?"

Dr. DAVIS said, "…Before the real estate brokers could buy the prime property they had to deposit the finances for the two survivors… because of their young age, and their father owned his, and his children's apartments… that in itself amounts to millions… the brokers wanted that particular six square city blocks badly."

Dr. DAVIS said, "We've done tests after tests and came to one conclusion… the element that's introduced is heat activated."

Dr. Chrysler continues, saying, "That's true this cocktail is heat sensitive, tasteless and odorless… the chilled wine when warmed by body heat it is activated causing coagulation of the blood and death is certain in a matter of minutes."

GEORGE said, "Anything else doc…?"

"Imagine the patience it took to know the dead, their hobbies where they lived, professions where they worked all their movements… everything about them their likes and dislikes, what they ate or drank." DR. Chrysler answered.

TOM replied, "Thanks doc… we've got our work cut out for us… there are no fingerprints… the place was as clean as a whistle, no dirty dishes, no trash or throw away food…nothing… … except for the vomit on the carpet."

DR.DAVIS said, "That's where we found what they all ate, and drank for the evening…. I don't envy you your job on this one… the grudge could have taken years… you'll have to look carefully into their past."

GEORGE said, "We have the one who vomited… his life is hanging on by a thread… they had to resuscitate him more than once."

"Let's hope he lives…maybe he could tell us something that might help." TOM added.

DR. DAVIS said as they left the room…"I'll be in touch."

HOURS LATER….

GEORGE answered the cell phone saying, "Seventy Ninth prescient… how can I help you?" He listens then said, "Don't touch anything close the door… someone will be there … I'm on the way." hangs up and said, "TOM we have two more… and one extra body that was garroted… Let's go."

INT: GRANT AND ASSCIATES- DAY

All are gathered at the conference table, reading from folders… The Grant children are exploring various sections of interests, asking questions,"Does God really like you?"

FITZ nods his head.

Another child, ask."Does he really live in the sky?"

LIV says, "Dear… have you been talking religion again?"

FITZ laughing said, "It's working too."

THE third child asked, "Is it raining there all the time… it rains a lot here."

 One child falls down all laughs hardily…the nurse arrives smiling announcing, "Kids lunch is ready all your favorites."

The laughter continues…until one child says loudly, "No… don't want to go…"

The other children stopped at attention…

CHILD number two looks up saying, "Uh ooooh."

CHILD number three said, "Ooooooop."

FIRST child said loudly. "I don't want to eat!"

FITZs voice is firm saying "Fitzgerald Thomas YOU all of you will go with Nurse James, and you will apologize to your nurse …. She has prepared your favorite lunch… You all will go and we will talk tonight… understood?"

Everyone in the room sat in amused silence.

The children spoke at once, saying "Yes dear."

FITZGERALD THOMAS a tear rolled down one cheek, ask, "Can we talk tonight dear?"

FITZ seeing the tear answered, saying "Don't cry honey "…he asks, "Can we a have a big group hug until then…" the kids came with out stretched arms for their hug, Fitz continues, "After you've apologized and had lunch…we'll talk… now go with Nurse James."

They all leave the room saying, "I apologize Nurse James, "She hugged Fitzgerald Thomas …he continued, "Bye dear."

LIV looked on laughing said, "Your fault 'dear'."

HUCK snickers saying, "Yes dear…at least that's an original…"

Momentarily:

A light knock sounded on the door and a tall obviously mixed race man entered.

His clothes fit his tall athletic physique like an elegant glove…his skin touched by the sun, with curly hair trimmed to crown his handsome face… his hypnotic stare covered the room in one sweeping look.

Grant and Associates stared in awe and curiosity.

LIVs eyes lit, she said questioning, "DILLIE?" she repeated…"Dillie!" as she walked toward him arms out stretched, "? How the hell are you? Look at you Dr. Dillard Chrysler I never thought of you as doctor." She met and they hug as long lost friends do.

DILLARD answered, "Yes little sis that's me, doctor times two of medicine and psychiatry." His voice is deep enough to be soothing.

LIV said, "Smarty pants…he seemed never to study always had - A's- dressed like a hippie.

Nothing like today… Car o line had to dress him… are you still bedding CAR O LINE?"

DILLARD laughing answered, "As many times as possible…she convinced me that we were the same species…so I married her… she's a psychiatrist too we have offices together." As they went to their seats.

ABBY, "Thank goodness…"

LIV ask, "Any kids?"

QUINN whispered softly, "Lord I hope so…"

DILLARD'S smile changed his face to more handsome if possible… Dillie answered "Yes two, a boy and a girl."

LIV said, "I want you to meet my Associates… the whisperer is, Quinn, the one in awe ABBY, and HUCK known as JAVIAR is in computers and last but definitely the first in my life FITZGERALD GRANT."

FITZ saying, "Good meeting you doctor." And shakes his hand.

DILLARD said, "A pleasure meeting you all especially you Mister President... I see you're reading my account of the killers folder… we need to get down to that…the police don't agree with me… probably think, I'm some kind of kook…but they don't have a clue either… They told me the car burned hot enough to melt metal that said; when this is all over I think we'll have the Scandal of the century that dates back ten years or more to be seen unfold..."

Dillard's cell phone sounds, he answers saying "Dr. Chrysler." listens, then says, "Yes…thanks." Hangs up…To the associates, says "That was the medical examiner… there are two more deaths…brings the number to twelve. The number involved in the bombing ten years ago… I must add, that scandal started in DE Kalb County ten years ago, was never solved, is alive 'til today, too many cover ups, too much power blocked the investigation…I say follow the money."

FITZ asked, "In your account …how do you know this ANDREW?"

"We grew up in DE Kalb, Andrew and his twin sister Andrea I knew them from third grade. Their father was Benjamin Vaughn…Uncle Ben was an herbalist … traveled a lot … Andrew went with him and knew a lot about flora and fauna of forests at home and faraway places. Uncle Ben had a small island in the Bahamas island chain near Biminis…I never had the chance to go with them."

LIV said, "Are you saying Andrew has the ability to kill twelve people and the Medical Examiner can't find the cause?"

DILLARD said, "I'm saying just that little sis…Andrew is brilliant, and know everything Uncle Ben taught them both."

HUCK asked, "You say Andrew is brilliant… what do you mean by that?"

DILLARD laughed and said, "I have to tell you a story. Andrew would become bored with his home room instructor… leave the room and go into the next class room. He and Andrea wrecked the curve in all their classes… they would read each other's text books and retained the information… Uncle Ben had patents on hundreds of product…you probably use his toothpaste, and many other things. That was Andrew and Andrea Vaughn."

LIV asked, "In your account you mentioned the news media had information about the raped WOMAN IN Mercy Hospital…were they trying to cover it up?"…how did that happen?"

"The Administrator of the hospital was out of town he traveled with his wife, four children and his office staff. They were found in an upscale resort in the Montana Mountains at hospital expense…that was mentioned in our folders." Quinn said.

DILLARD said, "I think Andrew covered the MAYORS office along with the town council with flyers."

QUINN read on saying…"COMA WOMAN RAPED AT MERCY HOSPITAL…PRODUCED A STILL BORN BABY" …she paused then continued to read, "There's one in the folder you brought…The good old boys in the Media, it was said they helped in the cover up by under reporting, held facts out of the news to the public."

HUCK replied. "I see what you mean. You want us to investigate all the allegations…right?"

DILLARD said, "Yes and before I leave… I have the latest taped message and the flyers in order." he places the phone on the table. A harsh whispered voice filled the room saying, 'Dillard…my sister is dead…" moaned with a catch in his voice, then continued, saying, "My GOD Dill she bled to death after being raped in MERCY HOSPITAL and delivered a stillborn baby in a pool of blood with a used condom. I didn't protect her DILL… I'll find the rapist… I will get him and take care of him…then I promise you Dill…then I'm done."

END OF THE RECORDING…

LIV says, "It's not clear…some words are not clear…but you can tell he's hurting and probably in tears…it's 'so' sad."

FITZ replied, "How do we know that's who you think it is... I agree with Liv…"

"Decades of listening to his speech patterns…neck surgery… was never done after the fires ten years ago…he disappeared after five years from the hospital… and then supposed to have died in a car crash… you might have read about it."

FITZ said "The police account is here… I read that…you didn't mention follow the money… that is where we should start…or may be as far back as it goes, there had to be planning…we'll look into that…"

"According to the Medical Examiner the car fire burned hot enough to melt metal and it was not possible to identify the human remains…" DILLARD answered.

LIV said, "Dillie you've given us plenty to absorb in one sitting … I'm so glad you're Dr. Dillard Chrysler my friend and protector of so many years ago."

DILLARD continues, "I have an office full of patients waiting for me …any questions, call me…thanks for listening to me…" pauses, then continued, saying,

"And one last thing…sorry… the nurses screams were heard the night Andrea aborted… a number of people ran to the room where they found the fetus and a used condom in the pool of blood and other fluids. Andrea had bled out…. Resuscitation was not attempted…now I'm done… When this is over we have to talk... or have a party would be better I like dining and dancing …I will bring Caroline and our children."

LIV laughed saying, "We'll look forward to that… you and Caroline yours and our children… that will be interesting…"

Everyone nods together.

Quinn said, "We will deserve a party and dinner is always good."

DILLARD replied, "Kudos to you little sis… triplets…WOW…I saw your triplets on my way coming in…"

LIV said, "Dillie I must ask you…"

DILLARD said. "So ask Lil Sis."

LIV asked, "What ethnic group do you belong to?"

THE ASSOCIATES leaned back to listen to their same questioning thoughts they were interested in.

DILLARD smiling said, "I will tell you what my parents told us…'we are a DUKES mixture of ethnicity I came out the Conquistador side… Caroline is from the Ethiopian branch… we claim Creole…I told you mine now you tell me yours… remember I saw your triplets."

LIV answered, "Fair enough….our kids are unique…they have different color eyes, brown, blue and hazel all have different hair texture ….I have three mixes and Fitz has several."

DILLARD said. "You'll never do that again."

FITZ smiling said, "I'm willing to try." As he looked at Liv with a lascivious gleam in his eyes.

LIV said, "He did that to me…"

"Yes and I would do it again…" FITZ said, laughing getting into the jovial banter.

DILLARD said, "Try…I'm with you …go for it Mr. President." His smile changed his face from handsome to more handsome.

 FITZ said,"DR. Chrysler it's been a pleasure…" stood to shake hands.

DILLARD smiling said jokingly, "Mr. President … I know you're not the Prez. anymore I like saying it… I'll see you and the Associates soon under other circumstances… and call me Dillard or even Dillie."

HUCK speaks up saying, "Dr. Chrysler I have to ask…Do you have a diet and exercise regimen…you look so fit."

DILLADR replied, "I don't follow an exercise or diet regimen… Our families are Creole and we eat foods we grew up eating…gumbo; pastries all the good stuff vegetables, fruit and sea foods are special… My wife and I play tennis once sometime twice a week…well gotta go."

He leaves the room with a smile and a wave.

All eyes were on him and his cool walk out the door.

ABBY said, "There's no way that man should not be duplicated on this earth …wow…"

QUINN said laughing, "I'm first in line..."

FITZ said, "Since the main attraction has left the room… may we get back to the business of the day…?"

ABBY said, "He walks like that actor, what's his name? Oh yeah Morgan Freeman…uses his whole body sexy…WOW."

LIV said, "He is kinda cute … I never noticed it in school… he was always goofing off…and he might be right about Andrew…he thinks he is still alive and attached to his sister as long as she lingered …even though in a real world she's in a ten year coma." LIV opens her folder.

FITZ replied, "Yeah I got the cute part…" pauses, and then said, "Now I want HUCK to go back ten years, contact CHESTER and the group… first Chester and CELESTE can find where the police are in their investigation the location of the rapist …I'm sure they did D.N.A. testing on the condom…follow the money starting before ten years ago…that Tipplers Club."

HUCK nods, saying, "I'm on it." and starts to leave…

FITZ continues, "Oh Huck …OMAR and JUNIOR can follow the suspected molesters trail… listen with his lip reading skills for any talk of where this nut frequented ask questions…call us for anything you find…don't over step your bounds, we want a conviction in this case …in your folders are assignments, report back when you find 'anything'…anything else dear?"

HUCK said, "I'm on it…" leaves the room.

LIV answered, "No… that seems to be enough for a start dear…"she pauses momentarily then said, "I cannot get over the money that was generated, mansions are going for one hundred thousand dollars, and that's holding fees. The other prices are beyond belief…but they could afford the prices."

FITZ says, "Tell Huck to look into that…Meet here later…say after lunch at two?"

INT: NEWS AT TEN – NIGHT

BRENDA KNIGHT reporting, "We are here to try and clarify, rumor from truth, about the scandal of the century…starting over ten years ago...Dr. Davie and Dr, Chrysler along with the DE KALB CITY, lead detective, who couldn't be here tonight but is with us via telephone… I thank TOM for your time…Dr. Davis reports have it you are not able to find the real method of the killings…is that true?"

Dr. Davis answered, "We found all the elements usually found in the body… but there is a triggering element we're not able to identify."

BRENDA replies,"What do you mean Doctor?"

Dr. DAVIE responded, "The killer has mixed a deadly cocktail…when introduced into the body it causes the blood to clot, there by clogging the blood vessels especially the heart, which causes excruciating pain and immediate death."

BRENDA turns saying. "Dr. Chrysler you have raised the argument that the killer is not a dead man… What makes you think so…? Against all reports to the contrary."

Dr. Chrysler answered saying, "The phrasing and the timing …I still think its Andrew …Andrea's twin brother… If you remember he heroically saved her from the fire ten years ago."

BRENDA said, "You're not saying a man is the killer…all reports say otherwise…a woman was seen leaving the home that night. You say it's her brother when it's reported he died in an automobile crash five years ago."

Dr. Chrysler replied, "I'm not saying it's Andrew but it seems like him, his phrasing…I listened to him for years as we grew up…You have a copy of the flyers, In my search… I found some of those and the place cards that date back ten years…same paper and print…the one thing that would bring him out in the open happened…the rape and death of his comatose identical twin sister."

BRENDA said, "We need more proof than that…We'll never solve this drama in thirty minutes… we will follow this closely as the news develops…we're running out of time … that brings us to Mercy Hospital. The Administrator has stepped down and is ordered to pay for the Junket with his family and all his staff. "

THE DETECTIVE, broke into the conversation saying, "That has been investigated and it was found the brother who disappeared five years ago was killed in an automobile accident that burned so hot not even the teeth could be harvested…we can't prove he's alive…it was not possible for him to live… the body was a cinder…no way…he's dead I would bet on that."

DR. DAVIS said, "The hospital is history…patients are being removed as we speak…their loved ones are taking them to other facilities…out of fear the rapist is still lurking around…no one will be left there but the cleaning crews."

Dr. CHRYSLAR, said, "You're forgetting the state inspectors and night watchmen are there…"

BRENDA said, "That has to be the last word 'til tomorrow Ladies and Gentlemen …I'm Brenda Knight…bringing you In the News."

INT: – THE FEED BAG LOUNGE - NIGHT

OMAR and JUNIOR had followed the grounds keeper …they sat across from the two men.

FLASHBACK:

ELMER HACKET the grounds keeper is a shy homely person, tall in stature middle aged man…and is a homely tall slender person with pale blue eyes…wears thick Len glasses…He takes a drink nervously saying, as Omar read his lips, "I went over to get my groove on and had just started when this bitch let out a loud moan… her hands moving all over the bed, and her eyes opened in a frighten stare."

HIS DRINKING BUDDY snickered questioned, Elmer did not notice the frowning stare "Man you got some nerve…Why didn't you leave when she started making noises?" the drinking buddy stared at Elmer frowning.

"ELMER never noticed the stare replied, "Nothing new she always moaned, moved her hands and opened her eyes…this was different, man there was a gush of watery looking blood and something else like a big blob ran out of her… I lost my condom…I had to get the hell outta there. Her moaning was getting louder and louder I could hear the nurses running in the hall… I just had a minute getting my pants on…and run out." he paused then said, "That was the second time it happened… I'm worried about that condom and D.N.A.….I'll see you later …I'm going home…I needed a stronger drink."

THE Drinking BUDDY asked, "You still live on Hoover…the Venice Apartments -1B-?"

ELMER replied, "Yes… you've been there…catch you later… I'm gone."

A figure of a man moves quietly through the bar and out the side door… following the grounds keepers drinking companion and heard him call the police.

THE DRINKING COMPANION frowning said into cell phone,"Hello police…? The grounds keeper is the one who raped that unconscious woman at Mercy Hospital…he lives at the Venice Apartments number -1B- on Hoover." Quickly breaks the connection.

The figure of a man stood in the shadows and listens to the phone call…he moves away and cast a tall shadow as he moved along the side walk.

INT: GROUNDS KEEPERS APARTMENT – NIGHT

ELMER answered the cell phone saying."Hello."

A RASPY WHISPER said, "You raped my sister… you can't get away with it… I know where you live, and I know you're every move you want know when or where… you can't hide from me."

The grounds keeper is consumed with fear.

ELMER dialed nervously, "Police you gotta protect me…! The brother of that dead woman at Mercy Hospital called me…! He just threatened my life…! The patient that died in Mercy Hospital he said she was his sister…! You gotta give me protection… He's crazy!!"

POLICE Man asked, "Who are you and what's your address…? I'll send a car for you."

ELMER said, "ELMER HACKET…Venice Apartments 1B on Hoover… please hurry! He knows where I live!! He just told me!! He's a killer… I tell you he's crazy!!!"

EXT: NEWS STUDIO - NIGHT

"NEWS HEADLINES Grounds keeper…for MERCEY HOSPITAL arrested for alleged rape of a comatose patient …His arraignment is due this morning in a closed session of superior court on molestation charges of molesting a comatose patient that bled to death and alone delivered a stillborn child…The news was scattered throughout the city last night by flyers anonymously…"

The prisoner was escorted out in chains… Kevlar protective body armor and surrounded by law enforcement officers.

.The News Media were mixed with the yelling crowd gathered along the street outside the court building behind barriers…the crowd yelled curses loudly jeering, shouted threats… shaking their fists…!

One yelled…"Can't you get a conscious woman… you're a sleaze ball rapist …?"

"Rapist of unconscious women you pervert…!"

"He's a sexually inadequate bum, cut his balls off…give me the knife I'll do it…please!"

The angry crowd grows louder… continues to grow noisier, riotous and throw rocks, cans, bricks and bottles… police in riot gear has their hands full trying to shield the prisoner from the angry ones…

EXT: BUS STOP- DAY

Two women sat waiting for a bus.

MILLIE asked, "What's going on in front of the courthouse?"

GERTRUDE replies, "Didn't I tell you the rapist of that woman in coma was caught…he is being arraigned today… the coma woman died while giving birth to a still born child."

MILLIE said, "Gertrude you lying! …you never told me about the baby… this nasty fool raped that woman in a coma! The woman we read about for the last eight or ten years?"

GERTRUDE said, "I kid you not… she is one and the same…I say they should take the bastard out and cut off his chocolate wiz-Wang with a dull knife."

MILLIE said, "I didn't know you were so brutal, but it's not enough for the bastard…It might be chocolate or vanilla… I could take him to the woods stretch it out on a stump and hack it off with an axe."

GERTRUDE answered with a laugh, "Fool you crazy… that would be under kill…he can't have that much to chop off… our bus is here."

Laughing…They gathered their belongings stood to wait.

EXT: FRONT OF COURT HOUSE –DAY

Elmer cringed in fear with the barrage of rocks, bricks and bottles being thrown at him…. The police closed ranks when Elmer tried to run…police has to guide him quickly to the patrol car!

EXT: COURTHOUSE – DAY

The crowd nearing riot frenzy…other officers has to be called.

MAN yelled, "He needs a horse whipping, and I to give it… the sleaze ball rapist, give him to me please…!"

"Hang the bastard he's worst than a mad dog…!"

"Leave the coma rapist with me just one minute…!"

"Castrate the son of a beach comber then hang his ass…!"

The crowd noises became louder, calamity ensued they had to be held back…

A lone figure stood atop the building a block away watching Elmer's progression through the yelling crowd until he climbed into the patrol car, surrounded by the angry crowd then driven quickly away.

INT: SAFE HOUSE – NIGHT

A note left surreptitiously on Elmer's dinner tray in a busy kitchen.

The note read…

"ELMER THE POLICE CAN'T PROTECT YOU FROM ME."

Elmer looks around then cowers in the dark corner of the room.

INT: GRANT AND ASSOCIATES – DAY

The meeting comes to order.

FITZ said, "Let's start with CHESTER…"

CHESTER walked to the board saying, "We followed Elmer to his home… when he went out to dinner …followed by JUNIOR he called us when his dinner was over…OMAR and I entered the house…up stairs we found the wall of shame…never touching anything…. We took pictures….I couldn't believe it." Chester and Omar attached pictures to the show up wall…the Associates were aghast as the photos revealed unconscious women all in sexually explicit positions.

FITZ looked at the wide array of pictures said, "This screwed up nut has been at this for a long time …Andrea is the only one with flowers…the others appear dead…"

OMAR said, "I found the filmed tapes of sexual orgies with some dead and especially Andreas… the only live one seemingly."

LIV said,"You'll need a strong stomach to watch…unbelievable."

QUINN saying, "How gross…you say sick now this is sick…actually I'm really grossed out… "

ABBY said, "I wonder what his parents did to him as he grew up …they had to be screwed up sickies- too."

QUINN said, "You'll need a shower after this filth…"

LIV replied, "Elmer could only be aroused with the cold bodies or half dead ones… Andrea was warm thus the flowers and he probably thought she was his girl friend…sick bastard."

OMAR said, as he placed the pictures on the wall, "Elmer talked about his having sex with Andrea… actually he bragged he was getting his groove on when her water broke and she bled watery blood and his condom with the baby."

FITZ says, "HUCK… we will start now with you….you said you had to go back further than we first thought…?"

HUCK answered, "Yes twelve years spurred on by billions in greed… I found one person who remembered the men that concocted their diabolical scheme."

FITZ responded, "I read most of it… tell us all, its very time consuming."

HUCK said, "There were six Real Estate Brokers who decided to get the property no matter the cost by any means necessary…the monetary potential of the six square city blocks…their projected earnings in the billions… they prayed on the vulnerable poor…where just a few dollars here and there to the needy meant food for their families."

QUINN saying, "That is so sick…They were sick greedy bastards!"

HUCK replied, "I ran into some nasty stuff, these people, if I can call them people…their only concern was themselves and the mighty dollar, they would cut your throat for money."

ABBY said, "What's the world becoming any way one can get over on the other fellow…who cares if they're needy…?"

HUCK continued, "The tenants would not sell…that's when the infamous six decided to literally blow them out…bribery plenty of money changed hands."

FITZ said, "…Enough of this pity party … we have to clean this mess up…I have a packet of accounting records from a man who died last year…His son sent them to me recently…the son is dying of Aids..his father was a very careful Accountant… many accounts are in this box."

LIV saying, "I went through the accounts … there is money in several banks off shore …it'll take years to find them all…it'll probably run into the billions… as projected by the first six realtors."

FITZ said, "Imagine this started over ten years ago… all that's happened, started with them and their greed for money."

INT: SAFE HOUSE - NIGHT

Relief officers for duty to relieve the shift…they find the prisoner Elmer has disappeared.

Law enforcement alerted state wide.

NEWS HEADLINE ELMER HACKET HAS DISAPPEARED from the police safe house.

INT: - GRANT LIVING ROOM – DAY

LIV stands watching their children as they played examining their surroundings, she said, "I enjoy seeing them explore…"

FITZ sensing her change in mood, asked,"What's wrong Liv?"

LIV responded, "What will happen to our children if we're not here. Andrew has fought for his sister for at least ten years…and it appears he has been right along with Dillie. You heard that despicable man Elmer has disappeared?"

FITZ replied, "Yes I heard…We have to try and make the world a better place for them to live in…that we can do our damndest to try …"

LIV saying, "FITZ hold me… I've seen so much negotism and man's inhumanity to man in the past few days it's always the almighty dollar… that's despicable…I doubt that can be done by us…you and I lost one another for a time…I don't want to lose you again…" as she hugged him around his middle her head resting on his chest.

"That will not happen again… you and our babies will be together for a life time…" FITZ answered.

FITZ and LIV stood in the circle of each other's arms, savoring their warmth, watching their children play, fall down and laugh as they stand up.

INT: OLD FARM HOUSE – NIGHT

Before Elmer's wall of shame…

ELMER awoke tied to a chair in the center of the room…he struggles to set himself free, saying, "What have you done to me…why am I tied to this chair?" Elmer looks down at his legs tied to the chairs legs…intravenous tubes attached to Elmer's femoral veins draining his blood into a bucket … Elmer screamed.

ANDREW materialized from the shadows switched on, the light showing the wall of shame saying in an eerie whisper, "I want you to be in a position to see your wall of shame, scream all you want…no one will hear you nor come to help…My sister bled to her death, along with the damned baby you raped her with… now it's your turn to bleed…it want take too long I gave you a tea I concocted just for you a medication causing your blood to thin, you can watch your life drain away shortly."

ELMER struggles in desperation then a cunning look covered his face, saying, "I am dying …but you need to know…She was the best piece so soft and warm… even unconscious…she was mine…. You couldn't have what I had with her…perfect." he saw the hurt he caused saying she was his… upset her brother, he continued saying with malice, "Just that once months ago I took off the condom…I wanted to feel her and she could feel me inside her…her eyes opened, she moaned and her hands moved, I held her soft hands it was the best…" Elmer's voice started to falter his speech was weaker, he said, "It was the very best… she was not conscious but she felt me inside her warm soft body…."

FLASHBACK to DREAM…

ANDREW saw his sister in his dream in agony …her eyes blinked; mouth opened with guttural sounds, her hands moved grabbing the covers… Andrew was shaken by the thought of Andreas helpless and no one to defend her…The confession hit her brother like a fist to the solar plexus….

 Andrew recovered saying, "You will never have another wet dream about her or anyone else again… your life is draining from your sick body… breathing is becoming labored now it want be long… you are struggling from air hunger."

Sirens are heard in the distance as they approached the farm house.

ELMER short of breath said, "The cops are here your time has run out, we both will die." he gasped for air.

ANDREW answered "I will stay and make damn, sure you never breathe another filthy breath."

ELMER said, "We both will die tonight…its called justice…"

"I'll see the sun rise in the morning…you'll go tonight…I'll make sure." ANDREW said as Elmer's respirations became more labored.

Police sirens are heard coming closer, screeching breaks, and tires…Officers converged on the farm house…

ELMER said gasping for each breath, "The police will get you they're here… you can't get away…" as he sank into unconsciousness…his heart beat its last from lack of blood flow and oxygen… the police forced the doors open as Elmer breathed his last.

Andrew stayed until Elmer gasped his last breath.

EXT: OUTSIDE OLD FARM HOUSE – NIGHT

NOSY NEIGHBOR had waited for the sheriff, saying, "There is someone in the old Vaughn farm house…no one has lived there for at least ten years…I heard screaming coming from there a while ago…"

Policeman said, "We will have a look…thanks Miss Clyde…Hey… you might have solved our case…that could be our missing Andrew Vaughn."

Minutes later, Police surrounded the farm house… more sirens blaring come to screeching halt throwing sand and gravel in their path.

Andrew, after taking Elmer's pulse, looking in his dead eyes, turned to run…an Officer yelled, "Halt…police!"

Shots were fired…Andrew went down… police examined the body quickly, saying, "Andrew is done for, Elmer is dead…call the coroner for both of them…"

Another policeman said sadly, "He is history the poor bastard, so is Elmer that's poetic justice the pervert bled to death… Andrew took good care of his sister to the bitter end… sad for it to end like this…"

ANOTHER COP said, "We watched those kids grow up…I hoped he would live after what that pervert did to his sister… but that's not to be…the good that happened Elmer was found dead tied to a chair where he was drained of blood, Andrew did get his revenge for Andrea, that pervert bled to death…

Andrew did it all I didn't have a chance to read Elmer his rights."

Another officer said laughing,"…Believe me you need the practice…"

HEADLINE news caster said, "Elmer Hacket died under his wall of shame…his death at the hands of a brother who loved his sister even in death…that's retribution ladies and gentlemen."

INT: CORONERS CROWDED COLD ROOM – NIGHT

At midnight a sheet moved…Andrew shoves the cover off and quietly and surreptitiously moved into the shadows and disappears into the darkness of the darkness of the back alley.

Morning came and the discovery of Andrews missing body.

Headlines scream… THE BODY OF ANDREW VAUGHN IS MISSING.

Dr. Chrysler asked, "What happened?"

GEORGE said, "He was dead… I laid two clean shots in the left side of his chest."

DR. DAVIS said, "George is right… no one could live with the amount of blood loss."

"See the doctor agrees." George responded.

Dr. CHYRETLER answered saying, "…By the way doctor…what about my big criticism Andrew was alive?"

DR. DAVIS replied grinning, "Yeah ….rube it in."

Dr. CHRYSLER said, "I don't think he's dead… you could not have killed him by shooting him in the left side of his body…ANDREWS apex of his heart is pointing to the right, he was born with DEXTROCARDIA' where the apex of the heart is pointing to the right side of the body…a doctor never had a chance to examine the body… no

 X-rays or definitive examination…he was wounded not necessarily dead."

DR. DAVIS said, "I'm done…I need a stiff drink." they walked out together.

EXT: AN ISLAND IN THE BOHAMAS – TWILIGHT

ANDREW stood on an island… at the top a hill… his left arm in a sling. He takes a deep refreshing breath, laughing saying in his whispery voice, "That was for you ANDREA."

FLASHBACK:

A smiling image of Andrea appears before him…as she appeared in life… they grew up together in school, family outings, their father… Benjamin Vaughn teaching them his craft…Andreas face fades away smiling into the cool of an evening breeze.

INT: GRANT AND ASSOCIATES - DAY

FITZ to LIV said, "We should get everyone concerned together…and contact JASON on the line for a tall ship and take us all to BIMINI in the

Bahamas for that dinner and dancing party…I haven't had a good dance with you for too long."

He whirls her around laughing…

 Liv squeals happily as their children looks on stamping their feet doing their dance laughing.

"Why can't we start packing now… to our song… I Will Always Love You." LIV asked as they danced in their own zone.

"Works for me…Let's do it…" FITZ replied.

LIV saying, "We think alike have a Tuxedo Junction party music…all the kids and families…put a wiggle in your walk." she hugs him around the middle happily.

INT: BIMINI HOTEL BALLROOM – NIGHT

ORCHESTRA PLAYING TUXEDO JUNCTION …the gaiety and dancing has begun.

FITZ and LIV dance up close and personal to an old song "STRING OF PEARLS"… in their own romantic zone.

Dr. Chrysler and his wife CAROLINE made a spectacular couple as they danced with smooth rhythmic moves to Day and Night…You are the one…

CHESTER and CELESTE did their own moves to a beautiful Ballroom.

The night went on as others do their favorite dance moves.

THE END…

Story by: Imogene Grant

@imogenegrant3